Groundwood Books / House of Anansi Press
110 Spadina Avenue, Suite 801
Toronto, Ontario M5V 2K4
Distributed in the USA by Publishers Group West
1700 Fourth Street, Berkeley, CA 94710

ONTARIO ARTS COUNCIL
CONSEIL DES ARTS DE L'ONTARIO

We acknowledge for their financial support of our
publishing program the Canada Council for the Arts, the
Government of Canada through the Book Publishing
Industry Development Program (BPIDP) and the Ontario
Arts Council.

Library and Archives Canada Cataloging in Publication
Brébeuf, Jean de, Saint, 1593-1649.
The Huron carol / original version by Jean de Brébeuf;
English lyrics by Jesse Edgar Middleton; pictures by Ian
Wallace.
ISBN-13: 978-0-88899-711-1
ISBN-10: 0-88899-711-6
1. Carols, Huron–Texts–Juvenile literature. 2. Jesus
Christ–Nativity–Songs and music–Texts. 3. Christmas
music–Texts–Juvenile literature. 4. Sacred songs–Texts.
I. Middleton, J.E. (Jesse Edgar), 1872-1960. II. Wallace,
Ian. III. Title. IV. Title: Jesous ahatonhia.
PZ8.3.B74Hu 2006   j782.28'1723'0268   C2006-900250-9

Printed and bound in China

The illustrations are in watercolor.

To my friend, Virginia

THE HURON CAROL

Original version by Father Jean de Brébeuf • *English lyrics by* Jesse Edgar Middleton

Pictures by Ian Wallace

GROUNDWOOD BOOKS   HOUSE OF ANANSI PRESS   TORONTO   BERKELEY

'Twas in the moon of wintertime

when all the birds had fled,

that mighty Gitchi Manitou

sent angel choirs instead.

Before their light the stars grew dim,

and wand'ring hunters heard the hymn:

"Jesus, your king, is born.

Jesus is born. In excelsis gloria!"

Within a lodge of broken bark the tender babe was found.

A ragged robe of rabbit skin enwrapped his beauty 'round.

And as the hunter braves drew nigh, the angel song rang loud

and high: "Jesus, your king, is born. Jesus is born. In excelsis gloria!"

The earliest moon of wintertime is not so round and fair

as was the ring of glory on the helpless infant there.

While chiefs from far before him knelt

with gifts of fox and beaver pelt.

"Jesus, your king, is born.

Jesus is born. In excelsis gloria!"

O children of the forest free,

O sons of Manitou,

the holy child of earth and heaven

is born today for you.

Come, kneel before the radiant boy

who brings you beauty, peace and joy.

"Jesus, your king, is born.

Jesus is born. In excelsis gloria!"

THE HURON CAROL

'Twas in the moon of win-ter-time When
Chré-tiens, pre-nez cou-ra-ge, Jé-
Es-ten-ni-a-lon de tson-ou-e Je-

all the birds had fled, That might-y Git-chi Man-i-tou sent
sus Sau-veur est né! Du mat-in les ou-vra-ges à
sous a-ha-ton-hia. On-naou-a-te-ou-a d'o-ki N'on-

an-gel choirs in-stead; Be-fore their light the stars grew dim, and
ja-mais sont rui-nés. Quand il chan-te mer-veil-le, à
ouan-da-skoua-en-tak. En-non-chien skou-a-tri-ho-tat, N'on-

wan-d'ring hunt-ers heard the hymn:___ "Je-sus, your king, is born.
ces trou-blants ap-pas,___ Ne pre-tez plus l'or-eille:
ou-an-di-lon-ra-cha-tha.___ Je-sous a-ha-ton-hia,

Je-sus is born. In ex-cel-sis glo-ri-a!"
"Jé-sus est né. In ex-cel-sis glo-ri-a!"
Je-sous a-ha-ton-hi-a!

2. Within a lodge of broken bark
The tender babe was found.
A ragged robe of rabbit skin
Enwrapped his beauty 'round.
And as the hunter braves drew nigh,
The angel song rang loud and high:
"Jesus, your king, is born.
Jesus is born. In excelsis gloria!"

3. The earliest moon of wintertime
Is not so round and fair
As was the ring of glory
On the helpless infant there.
While chiefs from far before him knelt
With gifts of fox and beaver pelt.
"Jesus, your king, is born.
Jesus is born. In excelsis gloria!"

4. O children of the forest free,
O sons of Manitou,
The holy child of earth and heaven
Is born today for you.
Come, kneel before the radiant boy
Who brings you beauty, peace and joy.
"Jesus, your king, is born.
Jesus is born. In excelsis gloria!"

THE ORIGINAL version of "The Huron Carol," in the old Huron language, was written circa 1641, most likely by Father Jean de Brébeuf, a French Jesuit missionary. Father Brébeuf lived among the Huron, or Ouendat, people near what is now Midland, Ontario, for many years, where he worked to convert them to Christianity. He became fluent in Huron and wrote the first Huron dictionary. He also recorded vivid descriptions of Huron life and culture before epidemics, massacres and war changed their world forever. His writings are invaluable for the picture they give us of Huron life at that time.

Father Brébeuf was tortured and killed when the traditional enemies of the Huron, the Iroquois, allied with the Dutch and British in North America, attacked the Huron village of Saint-Louis in 1649. The Hurons had always been allied with the French. Following the Iroquois attack, the Hurons fled – some fled to nearby islands, some sought refuge with other native nations and still others journeyed to Quebec. At that time France, Britain and Holland, the colonial occupiers of North America, were in a struggle to see who could gain control of the whole territory. Native North Americans paid a terrible price for the occupation of their lands and for the struggle between the European powers.

But Father Brébeuf's hymn survived and was passed on from generation to generation. It was called "Jesous Ahatonhia" or "Jesus Is Born" and was sung to the melody of a traditional French carol. In 1926 Jesse Edgar Middleton, a Canadian writer inspired by Brébeuf, wrote his own version of the carol. In it he sets the Christmas story among the Hurons, giving us the beautiful and very Canadian carol that appears in this book. We have included Middleton's version, a French version and the Huron version attributed to Father Brébeuf with the music.

"The Huron Carol," in all its versions, is a part of our history. Despite the many tragic aspects of how it came to be, this song has come to represent a respectful, loving tribute to the Ouendat people.